THE BOXCAR CHILDREN ®

CREATED BY
GERTRUDE CHANDLER WARNER

BOOK

161

THE RAPTOR RESCUE

D0039442

ILLUSTRATED BY
ANTHONY VanARSDALE

ALBERT WHITMAN & COMPANY
CHICAGO, ILLINOIS

Copyright © 2022 by Albert Whitman & Company
First published in the United States of America
in 2022 by Albert Whitman & Company

ISBN 978-0-8075-1012-4 (hardcover)
ISBN 978-0-8075-1013-1 (paperback)
ISBN 978-0-8075-1014-8 (ebook)

THE BOXCAR CHILDREN® is a registered
trademark of Albert Whitman & Company.

Printed in the United States of America
10 9 8 7 6 5 4 3 2 1 LB 26 25 24 23 22

Illustrations by Anthony VanArsdale

Visit The Boxcar Children® online at www.boxcarchildren.com.
For more information about Albert Whitman & Company,
visit our website at www.albertwhitman.com.

Contents

The Eagle Cam

"Look, the eagle is biting his feathers," said six-year-old Benny Alden. He was in the boxcar watching a video livestream of a bald eagle. On-screen, the eagle held out one wing and ran its beak along its feathers.

Benny's sister Jessie leaned over her brother's shoulder. "Birds do that to keep their feathers clean and smooth. It's called preening." Jessie was twelve. She liked learning new things and often took notes in the notebook she carried everywhere.

"I love the eagle cam," Benny said. "It's like being at the nest."

Violet joined them. "I like it best when there are babies in the nest."

1

"It's not baby season right now though," Benny said. "Anyway, this camera is set up at a rescue center for raptors." He'd recently learned that a raptor was a bird of prey, a large bird that ate meat. "The rescue center takes in birds that are hurt or sick."

"What happened to this eagle?" Violet asked. She was ten and loved to learn about animals.

"His name is Pierce," Benny said. "He got in a fight with another eagle. Then he got stuck in a tree with a stick through his wing. They had to call the fire department to bring a big ladder! A woman went up the ladder, wrapped Pierce in a blanket, and got him down. It was very exciting." Benny was the youngest of the Alden siblings. Usually everyone else knew more than he did. He liked being able to share something he knew.

Violet studied the video. "He looks okay now."

Benny nodded. "They had a vet...vet..."

"Veterinarian," Jessie said.

"Right!" Benny grinned. "A vet-er-i-nar-i-an sewed up the wing. They'll release Pierce in a couple weeks if he can fly again. If he can't fly anymore, he

has to stay at the Raptor Rehab Center forever."

Jessie looked at the chat window next to the video feed. "A lot of people are watching," she said. "It says thirty-seven people are online right now."

"Pierce has a lot of fans," Benny said. "He might be the most popular eagle in the whole world!"

Jessie read the chat comments. Maybe she would learn something new about eagles. "I don't understand the comments from the user named Sebhawk." Jessie scrolled back in the chat. "Here's the start, I think. Sebhawk says Pierce is in danger at the rescue center. But the rescue center is supposed to get Pierce out of danger."

Jessie scrolled down the comments. "Sebhawk doesn't really say why they think Pierce is in danger. They just say Raptor Rehab needs better security."

"What kind of security would you need at a raptor center?" Violet asked.

"Do you think they need security guards?" Benny laughed. "Maybe the birds should be the guards! Eagles have big beaks and claws. You could give Pierce a uniform, and he could walk around the rescue, keeping out bad guys."

"Their claws are called talons," Jessie said. "You're right. They are very strong and sharp. Birds of prey use their talons to grab food when they hunt. Then they use their sharp beaks to tear apart their food."

"Does the person in the chat think someone will steal one of the birds?" Violet asked. "Surely it would be too dangerous."

"I would not want to get that close to an eagle," Jessie said. "The people who do the rescues must be very brave." She read some more of the chat. "OwlFan seems as confused at Sebhawk's comments as we are. It doesn't sound like Sebhawk is worried about someone stealing birds. They say Raptor Rehab keeps the doors locked, and only the staff have keys. Sebhawk still thinks birds could get out."

"How can a bird get through a closed door?" Benny asked.

"Can a bird pick a lock?" Violet giggled. "Maybe that's another use for those big claws!"

Jessie shrugged. "I don't know. Sebhawk seems to know how the rescue center works though." She scrolled through more of the chat. "Some of the other people in the chat are worried now. Some say Sebhawk is overreacting. The chatters must make up their names just for this chat. They use names like LovesRaptors, WildBirds, SoarsLikeAnEagle. They sure are fans of birds of prey."

"Me too," Benny said. "I love watching them on the computer. It's almost like having the birds right here in the room with you."

"But without getting too close to those sharp claws!" Violet said.

The door to the boxcar opened. Fourteen-year-old Henry, the oldest of the siblings, came inside. The children's dog, Watch, pranced beside him.

"Time for dinner," Henry said.

"Dinner!" Benny jumped up. He glanced back at the computer. "Don't do anything too exciting while I'm gone, Pierce."

The children stepped down onto the old stump outside the boxcar and headed inside. The boxcar was their favorite spot to hang out. At one time it had been their home.

After their parents had died, the children ran

away because they thought their grandfather would be mean. They'd found shelter in the boxcar and had many adventures while living there. Then they finally met their grandfather, and he turned out to be kind. He brought them to live with him and moved the boxcar to the backyard. Now they used it as their clubhouse to plan their next adventures.

Over dinner, the children told Grandfather about Pierce the eagle.

"He's my friend now," Benny said. "I hope his wing gets better." Benny frowned. "Only then they'll let him go. We won't see him anymore."

"That's for the best," Henry said.

Violet nodded. "Zoos and rescue centers do important work. They teach people about animals. They take care of sick and injured animals too. Sometimes they help a species survive. But it's best when wild animals can stay wild."

"I know," Benny said. "I want Pierce to fly again. Wouldn't it be fun to fly way up in the air?"

Grandfather chuckled. "I don't know. I might be happier to stay on the ground and have someone bring me food." He winked at their housekeeper, Mrs. McGregor.

"You know that's not true," Jessie said. "You're always going off to different places for work. You wouldn't want to sit at home."

"Now that you mention it, I have another trip coming up," Grandfather said. "And it just happens to be near the Raptor Rehab Center."

Henry sat up straighter. "You said your friend runs that place, right?" That was how the children found the raptor cams. They had started watching after Grandfather gave them the link to Raptor Rehab's website.

"That's right," Grandfather said. "My friend Carmen Fernandez is the director. I met her when she was doing some fundraising. They always need money to buy supplies and pay for the birds' medical care. They depend on donations and volunteers."

"Volunteers?" Violet asked. "Do the volunteers get close to the birds? It would be fun to help, but Pierce's talons look dangerous."

"I'm not sure," Grandfather said. "They probably have a lot of jobs. Cleaning cages, keeping records.

Would you like to go there and find out?"

"Really?" Benny was so excited that he could hardly stay in his seat. "We can go to the raptor place?"

"I'll call Carmen," Grandfather said. "If she agrees, I can drop you off there when I go on my business trip. I know you'll be a big help."

"We can do whatever she needs," Henry said. "And maybe we'll find out why some of these people in the chat are worried about security."

The children all nodded. They could learn more about raptors and how to care for them.

"That sounds fantastic." Jessie leaned down to pet Watch. The dog put his paws up on Jessie's lap. She laughed and gently pushed him back down. "No begging at the table!"

"Do you think Watch will get along with Pierce?" Benny asked.

"I'm afraid Watch will have to stay home," Grandfather said. "He might cause too much of a commotion among the birds."

"We'll miss you," Benny told the dog. "But I'll get to meet Pierce in person! I can hardly wait."

Feathered Friends

A few days later, the Aldens arrived in Silver City. Grandfather drove the children outside of town. The countryside was hilly, with grasslands and forests.

Benny pressed his face against the window. "Is that the Raptor Rehab Center?"

"Yes," Grandfather said. "It's a big place, isn't it?"

The center had a large main building and several smaller buildings. Grandfather parked by the large building. The children piled out of the car and looked around.

"This is a nice place for raptors," Jessie said. "When they're healthy enough, they could fly away over the fields."

A woman came out. She had dark hair with streaks of white. Her smile was big and friendly as she greeted Grandfather.

Grandfather introduced the children to her. "This is Carmen Fernandez. She's been here since the center opened. You'll stay with her this week."

"Thank you very much for letting us visit, Ms. Fernandez," Henry said.

"Please, call me Carmen," she replied. "I know we'll all be friends."

Grandfather looked at his watch. "Sorry I can't stay and chat," he said. "I've got an appointment to make. Have fun!" Everyone waved goodbye as Grandfather got back in his car and drove away.

Carmen turned back to the children and pointed at the smaller buildings. "Most of the birds live in those buildings. We'll look at them later. Let's start in the main part of the center."

She led them into the large building. The front area had several desks. A woman sat at one, talking on the phone. A hallway led back to other rooms.

"Most of the work gets done in here," Carmen

said. "Daisy is full-time staff. We also have volunteers to help answer the phones, clean up, and schedule tours. When we hear about an injured bird, we arrange to have it transported here."

"What kinds of injuries do the birds get?" Jessie asked.

"Often they get hurt by flying into something," Carmen said, "like a car or truck, buildings, or fences. Sometimes we also get birds with gunshot wounds."

"That's terrible!" Violet said. "Are people allowed to hunt raptors?"

Carmen shook her head. "Absolutely not. There are strict laws against killing, harassing, or harming any bird of prey. But even large fines and a risk of jail time don't stop some people."

"But why do people shoot them?" Violet asked.

Carmen shrugged. "Some people might simply think it's fun. Also, some hunters think hawks eat game birds, like quail. They kill the hawks hoping to save more birds they can hunt."

Jessie pulled out her notebook. "Does that work?"

"No," Carmen said. "Hawks don't eat many

birds. They mostly eat rodents, like mice. Rodents reproduce very quickly. Without hawks, you get more rodents, and they eat bird eggs. Killing raptors actually leads to fewer game birds."

Jessie quickly took notes. "More people need to know that."

"Education is one of our biggest priorities," Carmen said. "You might think I spend all day hanging out with birds. In reality, I do a lot of management and outreach. We have to order supplies, pay the bills, and raise money."

"I hope we can help," Henry said.

"Will we see the birds?" Benny asked. "Pierce is my favorite."

"You will get to see them," Carmen said, "but not touch them. We have to be very careful."

"Yes," Violet said. "Those sharp talons and beaks look like they could really hurt you."

The young woman at the desk put down the phone. "Carmen, we have an injured owl coming in."

The children exchanged excited glances. They couldn't believe something like this was already happening so soon after they had arrived.

"Thank you, Daisy," Carmen answered. "What do we know about the injury?"

"He found it beside the road," Daisy said. "He thinks a car hit it. It might have a broken wing."

"All right, call Dr. Lauren." Carmen turned back to the children. "When we admit a new bird, it gets a bird card." She went to a desk with stacks of colored index cards. "Owls get a green card. This paper shows the information we need to enter. Jessie, would you like to do this one?"

"I'd love to!" Jessie sat and read the list of questions.

"We don't always know how someone is carrying the bird," Carmen said. "It might come in a cage or cardboard box or wrapped in a blanket."

"What do you do about the sharp beak and talons?" Henry asked.

"I use these big gloves." Carmen picked up a pair of leather gloves that came up to her elbows. "They're really thick. They will help me hold the bird safely. I'll also try to keep it wrapped in a blanket so it won't hurt itself more by flapping around."

"I think I'll wait over here." Benny stood with his back against the wall. "I want to see the bird, but I don't want to get close to its sharp parts!"

Carmen laughed. "That's a good idea. I'll handle the bird. Oh, someone is pulling up." Carmen crossed to the door and held it open.

A man hurried inside holding a coat wrapped into a bundle. "It's a long-eared owl," he said. "I found it beside the road."

Carmen stepped forward to take the bundle.

The man hugged it to himself. "What are you going to do?"

"Our veterinarian will be here soon," Carmen said calmly. "She'll examine the bird. Then we'll know what treatment it needs."

The man didn't hand over the bundle. "Why isn't the veterinarian here now? This bird needs help right away!"

"Dr. Lauren comes in twice a week to check on all the birds," Carmen said. "We call her for emergencies."

The man frowned. "That doesn't sound very professional."

Carmen kept smiling. "We're limited by the donations we get."

"Shall I start filling out the card?" Jessie asked. Maybe that would distract the man and he would calm down. "Where did you find the owl?"

"I was bird-watching on the west side of Turtle Pond," he said. "I'm an avid birder."

"The owl is lucky you found it," Violet said.

The man nodded proudly. "I saved its life, so this place better not let it die!"

"We'll do the best we can," Carmen said.

"I need your name, since you found the owl," Jessie said.

"Sebastian Hawkins."

"Hawkins." Jessie wrote it down. "That's a good name for someone who rescued a raptor."

Against the wall, Benny frowned in thought. The name reminded him of something.

"May I please see the bird?" Carmen carefully took the bird from him and eased back the coat until a face appeared. The owl's round eyes seemed to glare at everyone. "It is a long-eared owl."

"I told you," Sebastian said. "Raptors are my

favorite birds. I certainly know the difference between types of owls."

Carmen turned to Jessie. "Did you get that?"

Jessie nodded. "I put down long-eared owl and today's date. I noted who found it and under what circumstances. It has a line for the animal's name. What should I put there?"

"The bird doesn't have a name," Sebastian said. "It's wild."

Carmen held the owl like a baby. "If this bird has a broken wing, it will cost thousands of dollars to fix. We have vet bills. We have to pay for its food and medicine and the buildings. People who watch the live cams feel like they know the birds better if the birds have names. They're more likely to donate money to help one of them."

"So photos might bring in money to save this owl." Violet took some pictures of the owl peeking out of the coat.

Jessie tapped her pen on the bird card. "What's a good name for this owl?"

"How about Hoots?" Benny suggested.

"That's a fine name." Carmen nodded.

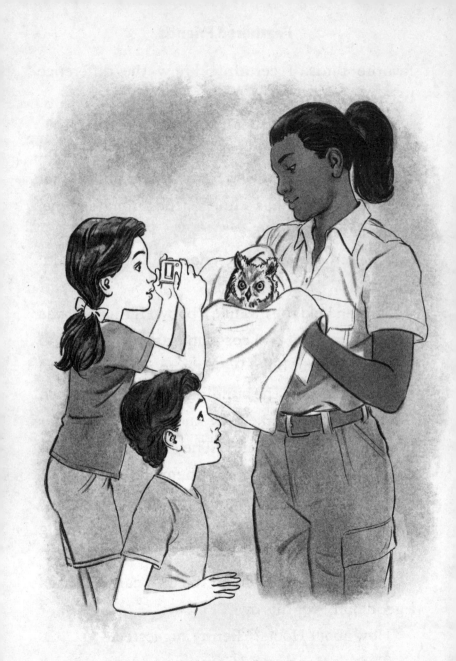

Sebastian frowned, but Jessie wrote the name down anyway. "That's everything I need for now," she said.

Carmen looked over the card. "This card will stay with the bird the entire time it's here. We'll update it and add notes about its care as we learn more."

The door opened and a woman came in.

"Oh, Dr. Lauren, here's our new patient," Carmen said. The two of them hurried down the hallway to begin examining the owl.

"I wish we could watch them," Jessie said. "It's probably not safe though."

"Are owls actually raptors?" Violet asked. "When I think of raptors, I think of eagles, falcons, and hawks."

"A raptor is a bird of prey," Sebastian said. "They hunt small mammals. Some definitions restrict the term *raptor* to falcons, hawks, and eagles, which are all active during the day. But many definitions of raptor include owls, which are nocturnal, or active at night. Altogether there are about five hundred raptor species worldwide."

"Wow, you do know a lot about birds," Violet said.

The young woman from the desk joined them. "If you leave your phone number, I'll call you with an update on the owl," she told Sebastian.

He grumbled, but he gave her his information and then headed out the door.

The woman grinned at the children. "I'm Daisy King. I heard you were coming."

The children introduced themselves. "This is an impressive place," Henry said.

Daisy shrugged. "Yeah, it's great. It could be even better though." She pointed at the colored index cards. "Look at these. It's such an old-fashioned way of doing things! We should have everything on computers. That way you wouldn't have to remember to move the card when you move a bird."

Henry thought about it. "It must be handy to have the card right where the bird is."

"Yeah, I guess," Daisy said. "We could do both. I have a lot of ideas for making this place more modern." She looked down the hallway and lowered her voice. "Unfortunately, Carmen isn't big on change."

"What else would you change?" Jessie had her notebook out, ready to take notes.

"We could do so much with computers," Daisy said. "An online calendar system would let us see who's scheduled to work each day. Volunteers could update it themselves. They could see which slots are filled and which are empty. As it is, they have to call around when someone wants to trade."

"Do you have a lot of volunteers?" Henry asked.

Daisy nodded. "Some have been coming in for years. We also have students who get school credit for helping. We need to track their hours so Carmen can sign their timesheets. That could be done on the computer. Instead, everything is paper all the time."

Henry frowned. "It does seem like a waste of paper."

"I agree," Daisy said. "But Carmen is afraid something will happen to the computers and we'll lose everything. It's like she's never heard of backups." Daisy glanced down the hall again. "But don't tell her I was complaining, okay?"

"We won't," Henry said.

Carmen came out a few minutes later. "Sorry about that," she said. "Let me give you a quick tour." She led them outside and pointed to a group of buildings. "Between those buildings is an open courtyard. That's where Pierce's enclosure and the eagle cam are located."

"Can we go see him?" Benny asked.

"Tomorrow, okay? I need to stay close to hear Dr. Lauren's report." Carmen pointed to one of the buildings around the courtyard. "That one is a hospital for birds with severe injuries. They have small enclosures to keep them from flying. Behind that is a building just for owls."

"That's where Hoots will go," Jessie said.

"When he's healthy enough," Carmen replied. "The last building holds birds that cannot be released. Some can't fly. Some are blind."

"That must be hard for them," Violet said.

"Yes, but we try to give them a good life," Carmen said. "We use them in our educational programs. Some are trained, so we can take them to schools or community events. They help teach people about raptors."

"That's good," Jessie said. "If people know more, maybe they'll stop hurting them."

"And if they know about this place, they'll know where to take an injured bird," Henry added.

"You have a lot of buildings and a lot of birds!" Benny said.

Carmen nodded. "And a lot of work."

Henry thought of Daisy's ideas. "Would using computers more make things easier?"

"I'm sure they would in the long run." Carmen sighed. "We're so busy right now that I don't have time to make changes. Maybe when things settle down. Lately it seems like everything is going wrong."

"How?" Benny asked.

"Oh, just strange things. Mistakes are being made, but I can't tell who's at fault. Some of the problems put the birds at risk. They might put people at risk too." Carmen managed to smile. "I'd better go back and see Dr. Lauren. Feel free to look around for a little while."

She hurried back into the building. The children looked at each other.

"Strange things!" Benny bounced up and down. "We're good at figuring out strange things."

"Maybe those people in the eagle cam chat were right after all," Jessie suggested. "If there are so many strange things happening, it could be a security problem. What if someone is doing all this on purpose?"

"We need to find out what exactly has been going on," Henry said.

"And we need to do it before anything bad happens to the birds," Violet added.

Henry nodded. "It looks like we have a mystery to solve."

CHAPTER 3

A Mysterious Mix-Up

Carmen seemed more cheerful the next morning. "How would you like to take a walk and see some birds?" she asked the children. "You can check on Hoots and finally meet Pierce."

Benny cheered.

They headed to the owl house first. "Hoots did have a broken wing," Carmen said. "Fortunately, the break was in the radius, a bone that's fairly easy to fix." She tapped her forearm. "That's here on us. Dr. Lauren stabilized the bone with a splint. Then she wrapped the wing in a bandage. It should heal well."

"How long will Hoots be here?" Jessie asked.

"Birds heal faster than people do," Carmen

said. "We'll unwrap her wing in about two weeks, then give her another week to make sure she's fully healed. If she flies well and can hunt, we'll release her."

In the owl building, Carmen led them to a small enclosure. They looked through the chicken wire at Hoots. The owl stretched her body tall and swayed side to side.

"Other birds of prey sometimes hunt long-eared owls," Carmen said. "The long-eared owls stretch and move like that to look bigger and scare away predators."

"Even with her wing bandaged, she looks dangerous," Henry said.

Carmen studied the card attached to the cage. "Wait a moment. This isn't right. This card is for a barn owl with a leg injury. How did it get here?"

They looked at other cages. "This one's wrong too," Henry said. "The card says it's a barn owl, but I think that's a great horned owl."

Jessie spotted cards on the floor and gathered them. "Here's the card for Hoots. Maybe it fell off. But why was a different card on her cage?"

Carmen rubbed her forehead. "How did they get mixed up? Why are some on the floor? Let's get these all to the right enclosures."

They matched each card to the correct bird. Jessie read the card for Hoots. "Someone added information last night after the exam. It says Hoots is fifteen inches tall and weighs eight ounces. That's only half a pound!"

"Birds have to be light to fly," Henry said. "They have hollow bones."

"They do, but that doesn't make them lighter," Carmen said. "Their bones are hollow but made of denser material, so they won't break. The hollow spaces are for air. Bird bones are like extra lungs."

Jessie looked at the owl, which stared back. "These birds are so amazing. Why would someone make trouble for them?"

"I wish I knew." Carmen sighed. "Let's check the other buildings." She led the way out.

"What's so bad about the cards getting mixed up?" Benny asked. "No one tried to hurt the owls."

"They need the right information with each bird," Jessie said. "Otherwise people might think

Hoots is ready to be released even though she just got here. Or they might think a bird had been fed when it hasn't been."

"I wouldn't like that at all!" Benny patted his stomach. "Missing meals is no fun."

Jessie smiled at him. "It's no fun, and if a sick bird misses a meal, it might get weaker. It won't heal as quickly."

Violet dropped back to join them. "Maybe it was an accident. A lot goes on here. Someone might have been distracted."

"I guess," Jessie said. "But why were the cards on the floor?"

"Maybe there was an emergency," Violet said. "If someone called for help fast, I might drop things too."

They went into the next building. Carmen glanced at a card. "This is the right card for this bird, but I don't think those care instructions are correct." She looked at some of the other cards. "A lot of them are wrong. Things have been crossed out or added."

"Do you have any new volunteers?" Henry asked.

"Maybe someone got confused and made mistakes."

"We do have a couple of new people," Carmen said. "Still, we don't let new volunteers update the info on the cards until they've been trained." She gathered all the cards. "I'll have to redo these."

They hurried back to the main building. Inside, a young man stood across the desk from Daisy.

"Oh, hi, Carmen," Daisy said. "Everything all right?"

"No, it's not." Carmen tapped the cards into a tighter pile. "I have to redo all these cards. Some of them have the wrong information. And in the owl house, cards had been switched between cages. Do you have any idea how that happened?"

Before Daisy could answer, the young man stepped toward them. "I heard you've been having trouble here. I guess the rumors are true."

Carmen frowned. "Who are you?"

"Faisal Raad, reporter. I got an anonymous tip about problems at the Raptor Rehab Center." He grinned. "What else can you tell me about the trouble you're having?"

Carmen frowned and shook her head. "There's

really nothing much to tell. I imagine one of the new volunteers made a mistake. We'll fix it."

Daisy piped up. "But if the bird cards were mixed up, one of the raptors could get the wrong medicine. That could be fatal."

"Fatal! Sounds like a major mistake to me." Faisal scribbled in a small notebook. "Have any raptors died because of your mistakes yet?"

"They certainly have not!" Carmen huffed out an annoyed breath. "You're exaggerating, Daisy. We only let staff and trained volunteers give the birds food and medicine. They would recognize incorrect information. In any case, we found the mixed-up cards right away, so no harm has been done." She added softly, almost to herself, "I'm sure those cards were correct when I left last night."

"If you had digitized the information like I suggested, this wouldn't have happened," Daisy said.

"Please, Daisy, not now." Carmen glared at Daisy. The young woman glared back.

Faisal made notes. "Outdated systems," he muttered. "Poor security."

"This is ridiculous!" Carmen snapped. "Everyone here makes the raptors our top priority. Most of our funding goes directly to care for the birds. We are constantly working on a tight budget and—oh, I don't have time to defend these silly accusations. I have work to do." She stomped over to a filing cabinet and pulled out a drawer.

Faisal grinned. "That's quite all right. I have enough for my article." He strode to the door. "My first big story!" he mentioned on his way out.

The children joined Carmen. "Have a lot of bad things been happening?" Henry asked. "Other than the ones we already know about?"

"I've already told you about everything," Carmen answered. "That man seems to think the situation is worse than it really is though." She lowered her voice. "He said he got an anonymous tip about problems here. I think someone has been causing trouble on purpose. They're trying to make us look bad."

"But you do such good work!" Violet said.

Carmen gave her a sad smile. "I think so too. I hope we can keep doing the work. Now we're getting bad news coverage though. Our reputation is on the line. We barely get enough funding as it is. What if people start saying the center should be shut down?"

"If the center got shut down, what would happen to all the raptors here now?" Violet asked.

"I hope we'd have time to make plans for the birds," Carmen said.

"Could it be hunters who don't want the raptors released?" Jessie asked. "Maybe they think you're making it harder for them to hunt game birds, like you said."

"It's hard to believe someone would go to that trouble," Carmen said. "I've tried to educate people about raptors and game birds. I thought I'd done a good job."

She pulled out some files. "Let's go to that larger table. We'll write new cards matching the intake information in the files." Carmen explained what to do. The children copied information from the files to the cards, and Carmen checked each card. The work went quickly with everyone helping.

"Is it lunchtime yet?" Benny asked after a while.

Carmen glanced at her watch. "It's only ten thirty."

"I bet Pierce is hungry," Benny said. "He's a big bird. He must need to eat a lot."

"Hey, that gives me an idea," Henry said. "You have the eagle cam in Pierce's cage. Sometimes it shows the helpers feeding him. Are there other cameras? Do you have security cameras that might show who moved the cards?"

Carmen looked up from her paperwork. "No security cameras. We do have other cameras pointed at birds, but they won't show anyone in the hallway."

Jessie pulled out her notebook. "When did these suspicious things start happening?"

"It's been about two weeks," Carmen said.

"You said the bird cards were right last night. Have you been having a lot of problems overnight?" Jessie asked.

Carmen tapped her pen on the table. "I hadn't really thought about it. We found the problems at different times of day. The events could have all happened at night though. We might not have noticed until later the next day."

"If things happen at night, the person must have a key," Henry said.

"Unfortunately, that doesn't narrow the field much," Carmen said. "All full-time workers have keys. Someone might need to come at night to take in an injured bird."

"But volunteers don't have keys?" Jessie asked.

"Not usually," Carmen said. "A longtime volunteer might get a key if they're filling in for staff on vacation. They have to give the key back after that."

"Could someone make a copy of the key while they had it?" Henry asked.

"Goodness, I'd never even thought of that," Carmen said. "In the last year alone, we must have had thirty part-time volunteers. That's in addition to the three full-time staff members, the vet, and a weekly cleaning crew. We have extra keys in the reception desk. I never thought to count them or keep track of them."

Carmen sighed. "Maybe that reporter was right. We really don't have good security. I assumed everyone here cared about the raptors as much as I do."

Daisy called out, "We do care! That's why

we want to make things better. I hope now you'll think about my suggestions. With digital keypads, you wouldn't need keys at all. You could give people different codes and track who went through each door."

"Great idea, but do you know how much that costs?" Carmen said.

"That's your answer to everything," Daisy grumbled.

Jessie and Henry exchanged a look.

"We need to find answers fast," Henry whispered.

Jessie nodded. "If we don't, this place is in trouble."

CHAPTER 4

Bad News

The following morning, the children watched Daisy give an educational program for visitors. Daisy put on one of the thick leather gloves that came up to her elbow. Then she opened an enclosure containing one of the birds who was a permanent resident. The great horned owl climbed onto her arm as she addressed the crowd.

"This is Al," Daisy said. "He's one of our ambassadors. We call him an ambassador because he represents us and all the raptors."

The big owl swiveled his head, looking at the crowd.

Daisy explained what a raptor was. She pointed out Al's huge talons and talked about his good vision and hearing. "Owls have special feathers. When they fly, they're basically silent. This is a big help when they hunt."

"Is Al your pet?" a little girl asked.

"No," Daisy said. "He is still a wild animal, even though he lives here at the center. He came here five years ago with injuries. He couldn't be released again because his injuries were too severe."

"What hurt him?" a man asked.

"He flew into a power line," Daisy said. "He probably didn't even see the wire. Collisions are the biggest cause of injury to raptors. They can hit cars, trains, airplanes, and wind turbines. They might even fly into a window because they see the reflection of a tree."

"Is that why most of the raptors are here?" the man asked.

Daisy nodded. "It's not the only danger though. Maybe a person puts out poison for rats or mice. If the raptor eats the poisoned animal, it gets poisoned too. Sometimes a tree gets cut down or blown down in a storm. If a bird was nesting in the tree, it could be hurt."

"What can we do to help?" Henry asked.

"Avoid poisoning rodents if you can," Daisy said. "If you need to cut down trees, do it outside of nesting season. Birds can also be poisoned by eating lead. A raptor might eat a fish that swallowed a lead sinker a fisherman lost. Or the raptor might scavenge meat from a deer a hunter shot with lead bullets. Then the lead can make them sick. People can use gear that isn't made with lead instead."

"Wow," Violet whispered to Jessie. "I didn't know how dangerous the world is for birds."

"It's sad." Jessie took notes. "I can hardly keep up. At least we're learning about the dangers, so we can help. We can take what we learn back home to Greenfield."

"Habitat loss is a problem as well," Daisy said. "We have to protect nature, from grasslands to forests. Fighting climate change is one of the best ways to help birds and all wild animals."

"What should we do if we find an injured raptor?" a boy in the audience asked.

"Call us," Daisy said. "We'll try to come get it. We don't recommend that you move the bird yourself.

Bad News

Keep your distance so you don't cause the bird more stress. If you have to move a raptor because it's in danger, be careful! Put a towel or some paper towels in a box. Try using a broom to gently sweep the bird into the box. Close the box and put a towel over it to keep it dark and quiet. Keep the bird warm, but don't give it food or water."

"Why not?" Benny asked. "Won't it be hungry?"

"Raptors have special diets," Daisy said. "You can't give it regular food, not even meat. Also, if the bird has been sick for a while, giving it food or water could kill it. Get it to a veterinarian or to us as soon as possible."

"She sure knows a lot," Benny said.

"She cares about birds a lot too," Violet said.

At the end of the tour, Daisy encouraged everyone to donate money to the Raptor Rehab Center. "We want to give our birds the very best care. Some things need to be updated. I'd like to install a new system to keep the birds safe."

"Like a security system?" The man who asked the question laughed. "Are your birds in prison?"

Daisy smiled. "Enclosures keep the birds safe.

Just last week, one of the volunteers accidentally left an enclosure unlatched. It turned out okay; the hawk didn't get out of the enclosure. But what if it had? What if the bird flew outside when someone opened the building door?"

A woman shrugged. "Well, it flies back to the wild. That's okay, right?"

Daisy's smile turned into a frown. "No, it's not. The birds are only released when they can successfully hunt. Some of our permanent residents can fly but don't see well enough to hunt. They'll die out on their own. Other raptors might need time to fully heal. If they escape, they could hurt themselves worse."

"Okay, okay." The man pulled out his wallet. "Here's five dollars."

A car pulled up. Sebastian Hawkins, the man who'd brought Hoots to the center, got out. He waved a newspaper over his head. "This is terrible!" he called as he marched over.

"Uh-oh," Henry said. "That guy looks ready to complain some more. Let's head him off before he stops people from donating money."

Bad News

The children gathered around Mr. Hawkins. "What's wrong?" Henry asked.

"This article describes all kinds of problems at the rehab center," Mr. Hawkins complained. "I shouldn't have brought that owl here."

"You'd better come talk to Ms. Fernandez," Henry said, leading Mr. Hawkins away from Daisy's presentation.

Inside the main building, the children stood back and watched as Carmen tried to calm down Sebastian. He kept asking questions, but he didn't seem to trust her answers.

"He acts like it's his own owl," Jessie said. "It's not a pet. He doesn't get to decide what kind of care Hoots needs."

"He wants to know Hoots will be all right," Violet said. "I would care about an injured animal I found."

Henry drew the others farther away. "He knows a lot about how things work here."

"Maybe he went on a tour," Benny said.

"He's talking about the daily schedule and feeding routines," Henry said. "I don't think that is part of the tour."

"Volunteers would know that." Jessie spread her notebook open on a table. "But if he'd been a volunteer, Carmen would know him."

Finally Sebastian left. Carmen put a hand over her eyes for a moment before joining the children. "What a day. We've been getting phone calls all morning. I'm generally in favor of publicity, but that newspaper article tore us apart. People who had never even heard about us before want to complain."

"Maybe some of them will donate money to improve things," Jessie suggested.

Carmen's smile was sad. "That would be the best-case scenario. I'm afraid some of our regular donors will stop giving money. Other people might try to get our license revoked."

"License?" Benny frowned. "Like a license to drive a car?"

Carmen chuckled. "Not quite. You can't keep raptors without a special license. Some people keep raptors for hunting. That is, they use the raptors to hunt other birds, like ducks. Some people breed them and sell the chicks. And then there are groups like us, who take care of them. We need our license to keep doing that. Otherwise, all our good work disappears."

"How can we help?" Violet asked.

"I'll probably be busy on the phone all day," said Carmen. "Daisy or one of the senior volunteers can let you know what needs to be done." Carmen headed down the hallway.

The children sat around the big table. They were alone in the room for the moment.

"It seems like the center could really be in trouble," Henry said. "People are paying close attention to everything bad that happens."

"There are problems, but they don't seem that bad," Violet said. "Could someone be trying to make things seem worse than they really are?"

Jessie bit her lip as she scanned her notes. "Isn't it strange that Sebastian showed up again? He said he's worried about Hoots, but what is he going to do? He can't take the owl back unless he has a license."

"When we met him, I thought of something," Benny said.

The others waited. Finally Henry said, "Well? What was it?"

"I'm trying to remember." Benny stared at the ceiling. "Oh, I got it! It was his name. It reminded me of something, but I don't know what. I wish I could figure it out."

"We said Hawkins was a good name for someone who rescued a raptor," Jessie said.

"But Hoots is an owl." Benny laughed. "That man's name should be Sebastian Owlins!"

"Maybe he got interested in birds because he had a bird name," Henry said. "I don't think it matters for our investigation. I wonder about that reporter. Why would he write such a negative story? It's like he wanted the Raptor Rehab Center to look bad."

Jessie looked over her notes. "When he left, he said something about this being his first big story."

"I guess he's pretty young," Henry said. "Maybe he wants to write a big article that gets attention, so *he* gets attention. He got lucky showing up in time to hear Carmen talk about the cards. She wouldn't have said anything if she knew he was a reporter."

"Daisy would have," Violet said. "She kept talking about the problems even after Carmen tried to pretend everything was okay."

"I wonder if that reporter wants a story bad enough to make one happen." Jessie found the newspaper Sebastian Hawkins had left behind. She opened it to the story on the Raptor Rehab Center. She copied down the name of the reporter: Faisal Raad. "Maybe he's behind the problems," she said.

"That makes sense," Violet said. "I can't believe someone who works here or volunteers here would try to hurt the place. But wait. How could the reporter have mixed up the bird cards? He wouldn't have a key to the building." She slumped in her chair. "Maybe an insider is causing trouble after all."

"We have to help Carmen," Benny said. "And we have to help Pierce and Hoots and all the birds."

The others nodded.

"One thing is for sure," said Henry. "All these strange events can't be a coincidence. Someone is out to get the Raptor Rehab Center."

CHAPTER 5

Eagle Escape

"I need to check messages," Carmen said as she handed Henry her keys the next morning. "Please visit the other buildings. Since you helped yesterday, you kids know what should be on the bird cards. Make sure they haven't been moved or changed again."

"We'll make sure everything is right," Henry assured her. He led his siblings outside. It felt good to get such responsibility.

First they checked the building for birds with recent injuries. Benny rushed to the cage where Hoots sat on a branch. "Good morning, Hoots," he said, greeting the bird.

The owl stared back with her big, yellow eyes.

Jessie checked the card. "This is right. There are new checkmarks for the feeding and medicine schedules. Everything else is the same as yesterday."

Benny looked at the card. "She got a frozen mouse. Yuck. But I guess she likes them."

They checked the other cards. A tiny northern saw-whet owl fluffed her wings and hopped along her branch, limping a little on her injured leg. A red-tailed hawk was much slimmer than the owls. It had tiny black eyes and a sharp, hooked beak. Its wing was bandaged to its side. The largest bird was an osprey. It was about the size of a goose, but it definitely looked like a bird of prey with its sharp beak and talons.

A great horned owl had soft-looking brown, tan, and white feathers. Its tall ear tufts stood up from the top of its head.

"The feathered ear tufts help with hearing, but they're not the owl's actual ears," said Jessie. She had done extra research the night before. "Many owls have ears at different heights on their heads. With one ear higher than the other, they can tell where a sound is coming from."

"That would be cool, I guess." Benny grabbed his ears. He pulled one up and one down.

Violet giggled. "It would look funny on us."

"Everything seems okay here," Henry said. "Let's go to the next building."

Benny ran to the door. "Let's go to Pierce's house next! I want to say good morning and make sure he had a big breakfast."

They went out a back door into the courtyard formed by the other buildings. In the courtyard, an enclosure housed Pierce and the eagle cam. A roof and three wooden walls protected the eagle from wind and rain. The other wall of the enclosure was made of thick wire mesh so Pierce could feel the outside air.

Benny ran to the mesh and looked in. "I don't see Pierce. Is he hiding?"

The girls stopped beside Benny. "I don't see him either," Jessie said. "Where could he be hiding?"

"An eagle is huge," Violet said. "We'd see him."

"His card will say if he's been moved." Henry went past them to check the bird card in a plastic sleeve next to the cage door.

The cage door was not closed.

A padlock hung from the door latch. Had Pierce gotten out? The enclosure door wasn't standing wide open, but it might have swung closed after the bird escaped.

Henry looked around the courtyard. No eagle. "This door is open," said Henry. "I think Pierce escaped."

"Oh no!" Tears popped into Violet's eyes. "He's still healing from his wing injury. If he tries to fly, he could hurt himself."

"Who could have left the door open?" Jessie asked. "You can't get to Pierce's enclosure without going through one of the buildings. Only staff and senior volunteers should ever open the enclosures. Someone had to get into the courtyard, unlock the door, and leave it open. That's either very careless or..." She trailed off.

"Or it's the saboteur," Henry said. "We'd better let Carmen and Daisy know."

They hurried back to the main building. Violet glanced all around as she ran. "I hope he's close by, but it's scary to think of an injured eagle around here. He might attack someone who gets too close."

"Pierce wouldn't hurt anyone," Benny said.

"Maybe not on purpose," Violet said. "But if he's hurt and scared, he might fight. Even if we find him, we'll have to let someone more experienced catch him."

They entered the main building. Carmen and Daisy were studying a piece of paper. "I'm sure I already signed this invoice," Carmen said.

Daisy shrugged. "I don't have a record of that. Maybe it got lost in all the stacks of paper." She looked over at the children.

"Bad news," Henry said. "Pierce is not in his enclosure."

"He escaped!" Benny shouted.

"Oh dear," Carmen said.

"I'll get the gloves and a net." Daisy headed for the supplies on a nearby shelf.

"We should have food for him," Benny said as he patted his stomach. "That works for me. If I'm ever lost, bring food that smells good. I'll come running!"

Daisy grinned. "That's exactly how we capture

eagles in the wild. You get a trap that looks like a fish. When the eagle grabs it, padded loops catch the eagle's feet."

"Are you going to try that now?" Violet asked.

Daisy shook her head. "Pierce is somewhat used to people. He's been fed here. Plus he's still recovering from the stick that went through his wing. He won't be able to fly away. I hope I can get close enough to catch him."

"If that doesn't work, or if we can't find him, we'll put out a trap." Carmen grabbed a pair of the long leather gloves. "You children can look for Pierce, but let one of us catch him. Don't get too close if you see him."

Carmen was quiet for a moment. "How did this happen?" she asked at last.

"The enclosure door was open," Henry said. "The padlock is on the door, but it wasn't hooked to the doorframe."

Carmen groaned. "Who could have opened the door? I checked all the buildings last night. I'm sure the door was locked then."

"You know, this wouldn't happen if we installed

those automatic doors," Daisy said. "I've been telling you—"

"Not now, Daisy," Carmen said with a sigh.

The women left the building, still arguing.

"We can't catch Pierce," Henry said. "Let's look for clues."

First they walked around the buildings. They didn't see any way to get to Pierce's enclosure without going through one of the buildings to reach the courtyard.

"Those buildings are locked day and night," said Henry. "But the staff have keys. The volunteers borrow keys when they need to work in one of the buildings. Someone could have copied a key and come back at night."

"Unless they got an emergency call, no one should be here at night," Jessie said.

Henry nodded as he examined the enclosure door. "Look. The door isn't damaged. None of the wires are bent. The saboteur didn't have to break in. They were able to open the lock. It uses a key, so it's not like they could guess a combination number."

"That means they left the door open on purpose," Jessie said.

"Someone intentionally risked Pierce's safety." Violet could hardly believe it. "Why would they do that?"

"That's a good question," Henry said. "Also, who is doing it? We need to find out fast before a raptor or a visitor is hurt."

"I'm worried about Pierce," Benny said. "He can't hunt on his own. He must be hungry."

"Don't worry, Benny. Eagles don't have to eat as often as we do," Jessie said. "They may not eat every day in the wild."

"That's awful," Benny said. "I'm glad I'm a human so I can eat every day."

They looked for more clues. They couldn't find footprints on the concrete of the courtyard. All they could find was a single eagle feather. That wasn't much of a clue, since it probably fell off Pierce when he got away.

They heard voices approaching. The building door opened.

Daisy walked in with an eagle perched on her

arm. It had a hood over its head.

"Pierce!" Benny said.

Daisy signaled for Benny to be quiet. "He's fine, but we need to keep him calm." She spoke in a soft murmur. "The hood helps with that, but let's not have any loud noises."

Carmen followed Daisy into the courtyard. "We'll have the vet examine Pierce during her regular rounds. Dr. Lauren will make sure he's fine."

Daisy went to the enclosure door and swung it open. She gently removed the hood from the eagle's head. Pierce gave a cry and hopped down onto a branch in the enclosure.

Daisy closed the door and locked the padlock. She turned toward the group.

"You found him really fast," Henry said.

"He hadn't gone far." Daisy crossed her arms, still encased in her heavy green gloves. "We got lucky this time. But what about the next time? We need the security doors. I know money is tight, but doesn't the safety of the raptors come first?"

Carmen's shoulders slumped. "Fine. Get me some prices, and I'll see about working it into the next budget. That's assuming we don't get closed down or lose all our funding before then."

Carmen headed back into the main building. Daisy followed her.

The children stayed in the courtyard, looking at Pierce. "I'm glad he's back," Benny said.

"It was lucky that Daisy found him so quickly," Violet said. "And she caught him! She's really good with raptors."

"We need to find the saboteur fast," Henry said, "before a raptor gets hurt."

"You're right," Jessie said. "We might not be so lucky next time."

CHAPTER 6

Questions and Answers

The veterinarian came that afternoon. She said two of the children could go with her as she checked her patients, but Benny was too young. They all loved animals, but Violet *really* loved them, so Jessie said Violet could go with Henry.

Daisy wanted to write up a budget for the electronic door system, so Jessie volunteered to take over the phones and greet people who came in. Meanwhile, Benny sat at another desk, having a snack and watching the eagle cam.

Jessie had time between phone calls to update her notes. She retrieved the volunteer schedule and compared it to the days when problems had occurred. She finished and closed her notebook.

They had some clues and some suspects, but they still didn't know who was causing problems or why. They needed more information.

The door opened and Sebastian came in. His eyebrows went up when he saw only Jessie and Benny in the room.

"May I help you?" Jessie asked.

"I'm worried about the owl I brought in," Sebastian said.

"I saw her this morning," said Jessie. "She's doing well. The veterinarian is checking on the raptors right now. If Hoots needs anything, Dr. Lauren will take care of it."

Sebastian shoved his hands in his pockets and scowled. "You make it sound good, but what about the eagle that escaped?"

Jessie was about to explain how Daisy and Carmen were planning to fix the door problem when a question came to her mind. "How do you know about that?" she asked.

Sebastian shrugged. "I don't like the idea that the raptors can just get out whenever they want. If they're injured, they need to be contained. They shouldn't be trying to fly. Someone could find the injured bird and hurt it worse."

"I understand," Jessie said. Sebastian had not answered her question though. Before she could follow up, the door opened again, and Faisal Raad entered.

"As soon as I heard about the eagle escaping, I rushed over," Sebastian went on. "I didn't rescue that owl for it to be hurt here or let go too soon."

"What's that?" Faisal pulled out his little notebook. "Tell me about this eagle escaping. And an owl was hurt here?"

"It wasn't!" Jessie stood up. She was still shorter than both of the men, but at least they weren't looming over her. "The owl is fine. It was injured before it came here. Now it's getting treatment. And Pierce is back in his enclosure."

Faisal glanced up from his notebook. "Pierce... that's the eagle that had the stick piercing its wing. Clever name. So it did get out last night?"

"That's what I heard," Sebastian told Faisal. "I love raptors. I was so excited to rescue that owl, but now I'm not sure I was right to bring it here. I want to make sure the center is safe, and I'm not getting any answers!"

The door opened once more. *Now what?* Jessie thought. She sat down in relief when she saw Dr. Lauren with Henry and Violet.

"Dr. Lauren, this man is worried about Hoots." Jessie pointed at Sebastian. "He brought in the owl and wants to make sure she's okay."

Dr. Lauren drew Sebastian aside and spoke with him. Henry and Violet joined Jessie by the desk.

Faisal grinned at them. "This place is great for my career. I was afraid the story would be over in one day, but it looks like there's more."

"I don't know of anything wrong right now," Jessie said.

"But an eagle did escape, right?" Faisal asked.

Jessie hesitated. Carmen wouldn't want the news getting out, but Jessie couldn't lie about it. Finally she nodded. "He's fine now though."

"Pierce didn't go far," Henry said. "The problem was solved quickly. It was really impressive. Everyone got busy as soon as we found the cage door open. They brought him back only a few minutes later."

Questions and Answers

"That's not very dramatic," Faisal said. "I bet the capture was exciting though. That huge beak and those sharp claws! Who caught the bird? Was it Daisy? Is that why she's not at the desk today? Is she in the hospital after the bird attacked her?"

"No!" All four children spoke at once. Henry nodded at Jessie to continue.

Jessie took a deep breath. "Actually, Daisy is working with Carmen on a plan to get electronic doors. They think that will be better security for the birds. It depends on funding though. So you see, everyone is doing the very best they can."

"Maybe you could write a nice story about the center," Violet said. "You could help them get more funding so they can take even better care of the birds."

"We'll see," said Faisal. He checked the time. "I'd better run if I want to get this story in tomorrow's paper. Tell Daisy to call me and tell me all about the exciting capture."

The children stood for a minute, watching him go. "He's only worried about himself," Jessie said.

"I guess he's only doing his job," Henry said.

"But it looks like the center is going to get more bad publicity. We should tell Carmen, but maybe later. She has enough to worry about."

After Sebastian left, Dr. Lauren went back to talk to Carmen. After a little while, Carmen and Daisy came out to the reception area.

Jessie told them about the reporter. "I told him you were trying to get funding for the new doors," she said. "I hope that's okay. I wanted to show that the center is doing everything it can to keep the birds safe."

"Excellent," Daisy said.

"As long as we can actually find a way to pay for it," Carmen said. "I don't want to make promises we can't keep."

Daisy took her place behind the desk. "I'll bet the publicity brings in more funding. You'll see."

"I hope so." Carmen smiled at the children. "It's a little early, but why don't we head back to my house? Daisy, do you mind closing up? I'm worn out."

"You can count on me," Daisy said.

They picked up some groceries on the way to Carmen's house. The children helped prepare

dinner. The meal was tasty, but Carmen still looked tired and sad.

Violet wanted to cheer her up. "The Raptor Research Center is amazing. Grandfather said you've been there since the beginning. How did you get started in raptor rescue?"

Carmen smiled. "I guess you could say it started way back when I was a kid. I found an injured bird in my yard. It wasn't a raptor, but a swallow that had crashed into the window. I nursed it back to health. Finally it was able to fly away. Seeing that bird take off and soar through the sky..."

Carmen gave a happy sigh. "It changed something in me. I knew that's what I wanted to do. I started studying birds. I read about them, and I looked for them. My father gave me a small pair of binoculars. I started bird-watching in my yard, at the park, on vacation. When I was old enough, I volunteered with a group that rescued falcons and hawks."

"That must be when you decided you wanted to rescue raptors," Jessie said.

Carmen nodded. "I like other birds too, but raptors really need our help. They have low rates of reproduction. That means they don't have very many babies. Some species breed after one or two years, but other species have to be at least three years old. Large eagles may not breed until they're over four years old. Birds with low rates of reproduction are at higher risk of extinction."

"That means they might die out soon," Benny said. "We don't want that to happen."

"That's right," Carmen said. "Raptors are predators, so they're at the top of the food web."

"I remember learning about the food web," Jessie said. "It shows how all the living things in an ecosystem are connected. If raptors are at the top of the food web, it means they eat a lot of other animals. Other animals don't eat them."

"Isn't it good to be at the top of the food web?" Benny asked.

"It's not really good or bad," Carmen said. "Usually, animals that get eaten reproduce quickly. They start having babies early and they have a lot of them. Rabbits can have several litters of babies in one year. Each litter can have up to fifteen babies. A single rabbit can have over a hundred babies in one year!"

Benny's eyes opened wide. "Wow! That's a lot of baby bunnies."

"Nature is well balanced on its own," Carmen said. "Animals at the top of the food web don't have many babies. They don't usually need to because they don't get eaten. Animals that get eaten have lots of babies. That way some of them are likely to survive. Things stay in balance. But people have thrown off the balance. We don't eat raptors, but we do kill them."

"But you said it's illegal to kill raptors," Violet said.

"It is illegal to hunt them," Carmen said. "But it's not illegal to drive on the highway and have a hawk hit your car. It's not illegal to put up a building and have a falcon fly into it. We harm them simply because of the way we live in the world. Half of raptor species are declining around the world. Almost twenty percent are threatened with extinction."

Carmen sat up straighter. "But we can save some of them. Some species are threatened or endangered. Of course we want to save every member of those species. Other raptor species, like great horned owls, are common. But I want to help them just as much as species that are endangered, simply because they're so wonderful."

"They are wonderful," Violet said. "I think what you do is amazing."

"Thank you. And thank you for your help this week too." Carmen covered a yawn. "If you don't mind, I'm going to read a bit and go to bed early. I'm worn out. You're welcome to watch TV."

"Don't worry about us." Henry pushed back his chair and stood up. "Don't worry about the dishes either. We'll take care of them."

The children washed the dishes and tidied the kitchen. Then they headed to one of the guest rooms.

"We need to find a way to help Carmen and the Raptor Rehab Center," Violet said. "She's been doing this for so long. She must feel like her dream is falling apart now."

Jessie pulled out her notebook. "Let's look at our suspects. First, Sebastian Hawkins. He brought in the owl, but he doesn't trust the center. Why? What does he have against the place? And how did he know the eagle had escaped today? I think he might be involved."

"How would he get in at night though?" Henry asked. "I'm not sure about Daisy. She caught Pierce awfully quickly. Was that just luck, or did she know something about where he went? She has keys and knows everything about the center. She'd know when the place was going to be empty."

Violet wrinkled her nose. "Daisy really seems to love the birds and the rescue center. She has all these big ideas and plans. She wants to make the place better. Why would she cause trouble? If she closes down the Raptor Rehab Center, she'll lose her job. I think she caught Pierce so easily because she's good at her job."

Jessie frowned as she made notes. "Carmen isn't as excited about making changes. She loves the place, but she seems tired from all the work. Maybe she should let Daisy do more. Daisy has more energy."

Benny sat on the edge of the bed, bouncing slightly. "Don't forget the reporter. He came in twice this week at exactly the wrong time. How did he know about the problems? Maybe he's behind them. Maybe he's causing the problems to make a good story."

"They're all possible suspects," Henry said. "I talked with Dr. Lauren today. I don't think she's involved. She only goes there when a staff member is present, so she doesn't have keys. I don't think she'd gain anything from causing problems either."

Jessie looked up from her notebook. "I looked over the list of volunteers today. None of them were scheduled on both days, when the cards were changed and when Pierce escaped. Most of them volunteer once a week at most."

"That was smart," Henry said. "Of course, if someone made a copy of the key and came in at night, the schedule wouldn't show that. Still, I think we have three main suspects."

"Now we have to figure out which one it is," Benny said.

Caught on Camera

Benny yawned. "My brain is tired of thinking. Can we watch the eagle cam? I like to say good night to Pierce before bed."

"I'll bring it up on my phone," Henry said.

He pulled up the Raptor Rehab Center's website and tapped the link to the eagle cam. Benny leaned close to the screen. "Aww, Pierce isn't in his nest. Maybe he escaped again! We should go back and look for him."

"Oh, I remember," Violet said. "Dr. Lauren took Pierce to her clinic, so the overnight emergency room staff could keep an eye on him. Since he escaped, she wants to make sure his wing is still healing properly. I'm sure he'll be back in the enclosure tomorrow."

Henry read the chat box next to the camera feed. "Some of these people are really upset Pierce isn't there."

"That's silly," Violet said. "The raptors aren't there for our entertainment. We're lucky to see them at all. This isn't a TV show!"

Henry scrolled back through the chat, curious about what else people had to say. "Some people agree with you, Violet. Others just want to know that Pierce is okay. I guess they heard the story about him escaping." Henry paused. "Oh no. Listen to this. The user named Sebhawk wrote a long comment complaining about the rehab center. They said it's not safe and included a link to the article that reporter wrote."

Jessie leaned over to look. "LovesRaptors is defending the center. But OwlFan agrees with Sebhawk."

"Sebhawk," Benny said. "Now I remember! Sebastian Hawkins. Sebhawk is like that but shorter."

"Benny, that's brilliant!" Jessie said. "With a name like Sebastian Hawkins, of course he'd use *hawk* in his chat name. I remember wondering if there was a kind of hawk called a seb, but then I forgot all about it."

Henry leaned back to look at his siblings. "Now we know how that guy knows so much about the center's schedule. He watches the eagle cam. He probably reads all the updates that get posted on social media. If you paid enough attention, you'd learn when the vet came and when different volunteers were there."

Jessie nodded. "If he took a tour too, he'd know where all the buildings were."

Benny clapped his hands. "Does that mean we solved the mystery? Is he the one causing problems?"

"Just because he knew everything doesn't mean he caused the problems," Henry said. "We haven't figured out a motive for Sebastian Hawkins. The reporter, Faisal, has a motive: he wants to get his stories published. He could also be following the eagle cam, and he could have taken a tour."

"Then there's Daisy," Jessie said. "I like her but she's the only one of the three who has a key for sure. She also knows more about the place than any of our other suspects. But we're not sure she has a motive."

Benny sagged. "So how do we figure out which one it is?"

"I have an idea!" Violet jumped up. "Maybe the rehab center keeps recordings of the eagle cam. We should check the time when Pierce escaped."

"Great idea," Henry said. "We'll have to make sure Daisy doesn't know what we're doing though."

With a plan, they were anxious to get to sleep so they could get started the next day.

In the morning, Carmen read the paper over breakfast. "More bad coverage," she said. "Today is going to be unpleasant." She sighed and put her face in her hands.

The children told Carmen their idea, and she immediately perked up. She agreed to go in early to view the eagle cam footage. "The footage is automatically recorded," she said. "That way we have a record if there's an injury when no one is present. At the end of the week, Daisy deletes the old recordings to save space on the computer."

They headed to the rehab center and arrived before anyone else. Henry fired up Daisy's computer. "We don't know exactly when Pierce got out. We know he was there at the end of one day and gone by eight thirty the next morning."

The video system saved the recordings in files that were one hour long. Henry checked the beginning of each one. They kept showing Pierce.

Then one showed an empty enclosure. Henry went back to the previous one and skipped ahead five minutes at a time.

"Look," Violet said. "Pierce was sleeping, but now he woke up. He's looking toward the door."

Henry let the video play. Pierce fluffed up his feathers and made a high-pitched sound.

Violet gave a little shiver. "I'd be nervous getting so close to that big eagle. The person must be really brave."

"But we still can't see anyone," Jessie said.

A figure ducked into the enclosure. They wore a hooded sweatshirt with the hood up. They kept their face turned down and away from the camera.

"They're avoiding the camera," Henry said.

"They know it's there."

Carmen studied the computer. "Lots of people know about the eagle cam. The camera isn't hidden. You could look for it before you went in."

In the video the person lifted an arm toward Pierce. The arm wore a thick, green leather glove that came up to the elbow. Pierce shrieked again but hopped onto the arm. The person put a bag over his head. Then they vanished from the camera's view.

Henry leaned back. "That was interesting. We assumed someone opened the enclosure and Pierce got out on his own. But they made sure he got out!"

"It must be someone who's familiar with raptors," Violet said.

"Sebastian Hawkins knows a lot about raptors. So do the staff here." Jessie wasn't sure she should name Daisy as a suspect in front of Carmen. "But what about that reporter? He probably doesn't know so much."

"It could be someone who knows a lot about raptors," Carmen said. "It could also be someone who doesn't know anything. Sometimes people bring in raptors they found injured. They have no idea how dangerous it is to handle one."

"Right," Henry said. "Faisal, the reporter, wants a story pretty badly. Maybe that would be enough to motivate him to face down a big bird like that. But he'd have to get a key and the right kind of gloves."

Carmen glanced at her watch. "It's almost eight. I guess we're done with the videos. We should get to work. Jessie, do you want to start checking messages from calls that came in overnight? Write them down for Daisy to answer unless it's something urgent."

Henry shut down the computer, and they moved away from Daisy's desk.

Jessie listened to the first few messages the phone had recorded. She winced as she took notes.

Daisy came in with a big smile. "Good morning! You're all here early."

Jessie put down the phone. "I listened to four messages from people who want to shut down the Raptor Rehab Center. They didn't leave names or numbers for a call back. I guess they just want to let you know how they feel."

"What?" Daisy wailed.

Carmen groaned. "I feel like my life's work is falling apart!"

Benny took her hand. "Don't give up. We'll figure out who did this."

Carmen smiled at him. "That's sweet," she said. "But even if you can figure out why this is happening, it might be too late."

"No, no." Daisy paced the room. "We need to increase the security here. That will stop any of these problems from happening again. People will support us if they know we're making changes, I'm sure of it. We'll get the funding back." She gave Carmen a smile that trembled a little. "It will be all right. The raptors need us. We won't close down!"

"Thank you," Carmen said. "Thanks, all of you. I'm going back to my office to think. Let me know if anything is urgent." She headed down the hall, her steps slow.

Daisy sat at her desk and took over the phone.

The children gathered together. "We have to come up with a plan!" Benny whispered.

Jessie bobbed her head toward the hall, telling

them to follow Carmen. They quietly trailed after the director and joined her in the office.

"What is it?" Violet asked Jessie. "Did you have an idea?"

Jessie nodded. "We know Pierce was let out between six and seven in the morning. We also know the bird card mix-up happened at night. We could keep watch overnight."

Carmen studied each of them. "You want to stay here all night? By yourselves?"

All the children nodded. "We'll be careful," Henry said. "We can take turns sleeping if we need to."

Benny bounced on his toes. "I'll stay up all night as long as I have snacks!"

Carmen thought carefully for a moment. "All right then," she said. "I suppose it couldn't hurt, and I'm not sure what else to try. Maybe you should all rest this afternoon. Then tonight you can try to catch the saboteur."

CHAPTER

8

Clues in the Dark

The Aldens helped out around the center that day. They also took turns napping in a back room so they'd have more energy at night. When the facility closed they went out for dinner. Then Carmen took them to the store to gather supplies before heading back to the center.

"Are you sure you'll be all right?" she asked.

"We have phones if we need to call for help," Henry said. "You worked all day and you'll have another long day tomorrow. Go home and sleep."

"All right," Carmen replied. "Your grandfather is always saying how responsible you are, so I'm sure it will be okay."

Jessie smiled. "We're pretty good at getting by

on our own," she said.

"That doesn't surprise me," Carmen said. "Call me if you need anything." She left and Henry locked the door behind her.

Benny did a little dance. "This will be so much fun! Look at all the snacks we have." He dumped out a grocery bag full of food onto the long table.

Violet paced the room. "I hope it works. If the center gets closed down, what will happen to the raptors?"

"Maybe we'll learn something tonight," Jessie said. "Should we turn out the lights?"

"Carmen said the light near the door stays on overnight," Henry said. "Let's turn out the others and stay behind the desks. Everyone take a flashlight and keep it in your pocket."

They chatted as it got darker outside. How long would they have to wait? Violet started yawning despite her nap. Benny ate a handful of mixed nuts and then curled up on a stack of blankets.

After dark, Jessie perked up as she heard a sound. "What's that?"

They all listened closely. "I think a car pulled up."

Henry knelt to peek over the desks and tables. "A car door closed. We have a visitor."

They held their breath. Outside, lights lit up the area around the front of the building, so they'd see anyone at the door.

After a minute, Jessie whispered, "I don't hear anything else."

"Maybe they went to another building," Henry said. "I only heard one car door, so it's probably only one person. Come on. Jessie, keep your phone ready to call for help."

They all crept toward the front door. Henry turned the lock and slowly pushed the door open. They were in the light now, but they didn't see anyone outside the building.

Henry led the way. The car was parked to the left, so he headed that direction. If the person had gone the other way, Henry would have seen them pass through the lighted area.

They went around the side of the building, moving slowly in the dark. Violet took Benny's hand. She watched the dark shapes of Henry and Jessie ahead.

Henry stopped. The others gathered close to him. "Look," he whispered. "Someone's there."

The moon gave enough light to see a man in jeans and a long-sleeve shirt. He wasn't carrying anything.

The children moved closer to the dark figure. When they were about twenty feet away, Henry turned on his flashlight.

The person yelped and spun around. The light shone on Sebastian Hawkins. He squinted in the glare. "Who's there?"

Jessie turned on her flashlight and aimed it over herself and her siblings.

Sebastian scowled. "What are you kids doing here?"

"What are *you* doing here?" Henry asked.

Sebastian shuffled his feet. "What's it to you?"

"We're solving the mystery!" Benny piped up.

"We know you're Sebhawk," Jessie said. "You spend a lot of time watching the eagle cam. You must have learned all about the schedule at the facility. Did you take Pierce out of his enclosure? Did you mix up the bird cards?"

"Me? I didn't do any of that." Sebastian scratched his head. "I am Sebhawk in the eagle cam chat though. I came to check on Pierce. He isn't in his enclosure, and I wanted to make sure he was okay."

"The veterinarian has Pierce," Henry said. "Dr. Lauren wanted to keep a close eye on him after his adventure."

"Oh, that's good." Sebastian came closer. "Look, I know I get worked up about the birds. I only want what's best for them. I would never try to handle a bald eagle! Have you seen the size of their talons? I certainly wouldn't let Pierce loose where he might get hurt worse."

"Well, someone is causing trouble," Jessie said. "If they get the center closed down, that won't be good for the birds."

"No, it wouldn't," Sebastian said. "There isn't another raptor rehabilitation center in the area. I want to make sure this place is doing a good job. I don't want it to close down."

Henry glanced at his siblings. They all seemed to believe Sebastian. "If you really want to help," Henry told Sebastian, "you could volunteer. You'd see how Hoots recovers. You'd learn more about handling raptors safely too."

"You could help more birds," Violet added.

"Could I really?" Sebastian grinned. "I've been bird-watching on my own for so long. It would be nice to make friends who love raptors as much as I do."

"Talk to Carmen or Daisy in the morning," Henry said.

The group walked back toward the parking lot. At his car, Sebastian turned to the children. "Thank you. I'm sorry I was snooping around. I'd apologize for scaring you, but you didn't look scared at all."

"We solve a lot of mysteries," Benny said.

"Well, I hope you solve this one. I'll be back tomorrow to volunteer." Sebastian waved as he drove away.

"He's kind of intense," Jessie said. "Still, he'll be a good volunteer if he puts that energy into helping birds. I bet Sebastian will love it here and volunteer for years."

The children went back into the building, locking the door behind them. They settled down to wait and had some snacks. Time passed, but no one else arrived. They took turns sleeping.

It got lighter outside, but the light was gray as it began to drizzle. Before long the staff would arrive.

Benny gave a loud sigh.

"What's the matter?" Jessie asked. "Do you need more snacks?"

"Yes, please." Benny looked through the remaining selection. "That's not why I sighed though. I'm sad we didn't solve the mystery."

"We made progress," Violet said. "We don't suspect Sebastian anymore."

"True." Jessie crossed out his name in her notebook. "But if Sebastian didn't cause the problems, who did? We don't have much time left."

"We just have to solve the mystery," Benny said. "For Carmen and Pierce and Hoots and everyone who loves raptors."

CHAPTER 9

Lessons Learned

The children yawned as they helped out the next morning. Carmen was meeting with the board members. These were people who oversaw the center's finances. They had to approve any future plans. Carmen needed to convince them things were okay at the Raptor Rehab Center.

"I feel nervous," Jessie said. "We can't help Carmen with her meeting, but we should do something."

"Let's walk through the buildings," Henry suggested. "We'll make sure everything looks right."

They stopped by Pierce's enclosure. It was good to see him back. Dr. Lauren had given him a clean bill of health.

Then they checked on Hoots and the other patients in the hospital wing. Violet took some pictures. "Hoots is really cute. I'm going to miss all these birds after we leave. At least we'll have the cameras to show what's happening here."

Back in the hallway, Benny ran ahead. He came to a quick stop and pointed. "Look, muddy footprints!"

"Those aren't ours," Jessie said. "They're too big, and we haven't been out in the rain."

The hospital building connected to the other buildings, so staff could move injured birds without risk of them flying away. The children followed the footprints around the corner.

A man stood at the door to the owl house, trying the doorknob.

"Faisal!" Jessie exclaimed.

The reporter grinned. "Oh, hi. I was just... looking around."

"How did you get in?" Henry asked.

"Someone let me in," Faisal said.

Henry shook his head. "Visitors can't wander around without a guide. Tell us the truth."

"Yeah, you shouldn't lie!" Benny said.

Faisal winced. "Okay, okay. I got in through a back door. I popped the lock by slipping my driver's license between the door and the frame. That door needs a better lock."

"So you know how to get in the buildings." Jessie put her hands on her hips. "Are you the one who mixed up the bird cards and let the eagle go?"

"Of course not," Faisal said. "I'm trying to solve the mystery."

Violet narrowed her eyes at him. "Really? You've been making the Raptor Rehab Center look bad in your articles. You said it was a break for you to get a dramatic story. How do we know you didn't cause problems to make a better story?"

"Wow. Do you really think I'd do that?" Faisal studied their frowns. "Okay, I see why you might think that." He chuckled to himself. "I do want a good story. When I heard about the problems here, I got excited. If I uncover a scandal, the paper might assign me other cool stories."

"Those are all reasons for you to cause problems," Jessie said.

"But I didn't," Faisal said. "I want to cover real news, not fake it. I didn't say anything that was untrue. No good journalist would do that."

Violet usually felt shy with people she didn't know well, but she was angry. She stomped closer to the man. "It's mean to cause problems for people who are doing their best. How will you feel if the center gets closed down because of your articles?"

"Could that really happen?" Faisal asked. "That wasn't my intent. I wanted to solve the mystery behind the strange things happening. That's why I'm here today."

He thought for a moment. "Maybe I went too far in making the center sound bad. A good reporter should cover all sides of a story. I'm sorry my articles caused problems. I thought I'd be helping this place if I revealed the culprit."

"Well, we do need to know who did those things," Henry said. "Have you had any luck?"

Faisal shook his head. "I've talked to the staff and volunteers, but if anyone knows anything, they're not telling me. I'm not sure where to go next. That's why I snuck in. I haven't seen anything strange though. Do you have any ideas?"

"We haven't figured it out yet," Henry said. "We are getting closer though."

"Will you write a good story if we find out the truth?" Violet asked.

Faisal smiled. "I think all my stories are good stories. Are you asking if I'll give the Raptor Rehab Center positive coverage? How about this? I'll try to be neutral. I'll make sure I give the director a chance to tell her side of things. I'll also mention how people can help by donating money or time."

"I guess that's fair," Violet said.

"You'd better leave now," Henry said. "The director is in a meeting, but we can ask her to call you later."

"Wait, one more question," Jessie said. "How did you know there was a story here in the first place?"

"Good question. Maybe you kids are clever enough to solve the mystery." Faisal hesitated. "I can't give away a source, but I got a tip from someone who knew about the situation."

Faisal left the building. The Aldens made sure

he drove away. Then they went back into the main room. Daisy was on the phone again, but she looked up and waved.

The children sat at a long table. "Maybe the reporter will give this place fair coverage now," Jessie said. "But we're running out of suspects. He says someone gave him a tip, but that could be any of the staff or volunteers. It could even be someone who watches the eagle cam."

"We need another clue." Benny rubbed his belly. "How about a snack to help us think?"

Daisy got up from the reception desk. "I need to give a tour in a few minutes. I'm going to greet people as they arrive outside so they don't track mud in here. Can one of you cover the phone?"

Jessie nodded and moved to Daisy's desk as Daisy left.

"Let's watch the eagle cam footage one more time," Jessie said. "That gave us one big clue. Maybe there's another one we missed."

The children gathered around the computer. Henry remembered which video showed the person stealing Pierce. They played it again.

Lessons Learned

"I still say that person is very brave to handle an eagle," Violet said, "even if they do have big, heavy gloves." She studied the gloves. "Wait a minute. Those gloves are green. I didn't notice before."

Jessie frowned. "Where have we seen green gloves before?"

"Daisy used green ones when she went out and found Pierce," Violet said.

Henry went to the shelf that held supplies. One tub had heavy leather gloves. Most of them were brown. Only one pair was green. "These gloves are available to anyone." He picked them up. "But I'll bet everyone who works or volunteers here has their favorite pair. These are pretty small. Not everyone would be able to use them."

Violet studied the gloves with wide eyes. "Did Daisy take Pierce out of his enclosure?"

"We'll find out when she gets back," Henry said.

Carmen finished her meeting, and the board members filed out of the building. Before the children could tell Carmen about their discovery, Daisy came back from her tour.

"How was the meeting?" Daisy asked. "They're

not going to recommend we close, are they?"

"I convinced them to wait," Carmen said. "We still need to find out who caused the trouble though. I don't know what we'll do if we can't stop the problems."

"Maybe it's all over," Daisy said. "Maybe nothing else will happen."

Henry held up the green gloves. "Does that mean you're planning to stop causing trouble? We looked at the eagle cam footage again. The person who moved Pierce had green gloves, exactly like the ones you use."

"You found Pierce very quickly," Violet added. "Was that because you knew exactly where he was?"

Daisy's mouth opened and closed. No sounds came out.

"You have keys," Jessie said. "You could get into any of the buildings, even at night. You know how the bird cards work, so you knew that moving them would cause problems."

Daisy staggered to a chair and collapsed into it. Her shoulders slumped. "You're right," she said. "I've felt terrible since I found out the bad publicity might cause the center to close."

Carmen stared at her. "But why? I thought you loved the raptors."

"I do! I didn't want to hurt any animals." Daisy dabbed at her eyes. "I only wanted to show how my ideas could help. I thought if I showed how things could go bad, you'd be more open to using newer technology."

"I was never against your ideas," Carmen said. "It's always been a funding issue."

"I didn't think you were listening to me," Daisy said.

Carmen shook her head. "I'm sorry if I seemed dismissive of your ideas. I've been overworked and under a lot of stress. Maybe I should have taken more time to explain why we can't do those things now. But what you did was not the right way to get attention. You put the birds in danger."

"I had Pierce someplace safe," Daisy said. "I was ready to point out the problem with the bird cards if you hadn't noticed them first. I wouldn't let a raptor get hurt."

"That doesn't make it okay," Carmen said.

"What if you had an accident and couldn't tell us where Pierce was? What if you hadn't had a chance to point out the mixed-up cards? And you caused such terrible news coverage!"

"Wait a moment," Jessie said. "The reporter mentioned that someone told him to investigate the center. Was that you, Daisy?"

Daisy nodded, then lowered her head. "I'm sorry about that too. I tipped off that reporter because I wanted to draw attention to the way improvements could help the center. I didn't know he'd write such negative stories."

Carmen held out her hand. "Please give me your keys."

"Am I fired?" Daisy had tears in her eyes as she handed over the keys.

"No, but I'm afraid I'll have to put you on probation." Carmen tucked the keys into her own pocket. "You can work the phones and do filing, but no more tours and no more working directly with the raptors. Maybe one day I'll trust you again, but you'll have to prove yourself."

Daisy stood up with her hands clasped together.

Lessons Learned

"I understand. I will prove myself. I truly want what is best for the birds. I didn't mean to cause problems."

Carmen patted the other woman's shoulder. "Go home for the day. Think about how you might make up for your mistakes."

"I can call that reporter and tell him the truth," Daisy said.

"Oh, we saw him," Henry said. "Carmen, he'd like to get a statement from you. He promised to write a more balanced article."

"I think I'd prefer to talk to him myself," Carmen told Daisy. "I'll let you know if we need you to confirm my statements."

Daisy nodded and left.

Carmen put one arm around Jessie and one around Violet. "Thank you, children. You really did solve the mystery. I'm sorry it was Daisy behind the problems, but at least no one was really trying to hurt the birds. Maybe she'll learn a lesson from this."

"I'll bet she did," Violet said. "I've learned a ton this week. I'll be sad when our visit is over."

"Oh, I almost forgot!" Carmen smiled. "I've got a big surprise to share with you."

"What is it?" Benny asked. He loved surprises.

Carmen smiled and shook her head. "Today has been exciting enough as it is. I'll tell you all about it tomorrow."

"Can't we at least get a hint?" asked Violet.

"Let's just say I got some good news about a close friend of yours," Carmen responded with a twinkle in her eye.

The children exchanged looks with each other. What could she mean?

CHAPTER 10

Wild and Free

"It's a party!" Benny yelled as he ran ahead.

The other children followed along with Grandfather. It had been a few days since they uncovered Daisy's plans, and things had started to get back to normal at the Raptor Rehab Center. They'd be heading home later that day, but first it was time to enjoy Carmen's big surprise: they were going to watch as Pierce was released back into the wild. Dozens of people had gathered in the field near a forest. Pierce's carrying case sat about thirty feet from the group. A blanket hung over it to keep the raptor calm.

"There's Sebastian," Violet said as she waved.

Sebastian joined their family and shook

Grandfather's hand. He looked happier and nicer now that he wasn't so worried.

"I did my volunteer training yesterday," he said. "I can't wait to get started. I'll be at the Raptor Rehab Center one day every week. I love watching birds in the wild, but it's also exciting to see them up close. Since I have experience with wild birds, they're going to train me to feed the raptors."

"That sounds wonderful," Violet said. "You get to work with raptors every week!"

Jessie looked around at the crowd. "Who are all these people? I recognize some of the volunteers and staff, but there must be thirty people here."

"We promoted the event in the eagle cam chat," Sebastian said. "People have been watching Pierce from all around the world. Some people came a hundred miles to watch his release. We also have a video feed set up for those who are too far away to come. It's a big day for all of us."

He turned to Benny. "Would you like to meet some folks from the eagle cam chat?"

"Sure!" Benny might have been the youngest of Pierce's fans, but he was as enthusiastic as any of them. He quickly made new friends in person with the people he'd met online.

Faisal hurried over from the parking area. "Isn't this exciting?" he said to the children. "I learned all about how they rehabilitated the eagle being released today. I have an article almost ready to go. I just need to cover the release today and get pictures."

"I'm glad you see how important this work is," Jessie said.

"It's incredible," the reporter replied. Like everyone else there, Faisal had a huge smile. "It's nice to cover a story about people doing something good. People need more articles with happy endings."

Benny rejoined their group. "I'm sad I won't be able to see Pierce on the eagle cam anymore."

Jessie put her arm around him. "He gets to be a wild bird now. We shouldn't keep birds in captivity unless they are too injured to survive on their own. The goal is to send them back into nature. Birds do best in their natural habitat."

"I know," Benny said. "I'm glad Pierce gets to be free. I'll still miss him though."

Henry ruffled Benny's hair. "There are other animal cams. Some of them even show eagles or other raptors. Also, we know more about raptor behavior now. Maybe we can go bird-watching and find some raptors in the wild."

Benny grinned. "That sounds fun!"

"I like seeing the birds in the wild best," Violet said. "I'm so happy Pierce gets to go home. Maybe he'll find a mate and they'll have baby eagles."

"It sounds like you've had a very interesting week," Grandfather said.

"We did," Henry said. "I miss our rooms and our boxcar though."

Violet nodded. "I miss Watch."

"Me too," Jessie said. "I can't wait to see him again. We'll have to bird-proof our house and yard. We don't want our dog to hurt any birds. We don't want birds to fly into the windows either."

"How do you stop that?" Grandfather asked.

Jessie held up her notebook. "I have notes. We can hang shiny objects from the gutters. Birds don't like them, so they'll stay away. Flags that move in the wind work too, and many birds don't like the loud noise of wind chimes."

"But we like seeing birds," Violet said. "We just need to make sure we put bird feeders or sources of water where it's safe for them."

"It sounds like we have some redecorating to do!" said Grandfather.

When everyone was gathered, Carmen headed out to the animal carrier.

"Look!" Benny jumped up and down. "Carmen is getting ready to release Pierce."

Everyone spread out in a long line so they could all see.

Carmen spoke to the crowd for a few minutes. She explained the importance of saving raptors and how the Raptor Rehab Center worked. Then she said, "I had some very special helpers this week. I'd like the Aldens to come up here."

The children joined Carmen. They waved to the crowd.

"Now let's release Pierce." Carmen took the blanket off Pierce's carrier. She told the children, "Crouch down in back. We don't want to spook him when he flies out."

They knelt behind the carrier. Carmen reached over to open the door.

The eagle hopped out of the carrier, flapping his wings. Within a few steps, he was airborne. He swooped into the forest. Everyone cheered as he rose up and down before finally settling in a tall evergreen tree.

"You'd never see him if you didn't know where to look," Henry said.

"We'll look more carefully now," Jessie said.

Carmen gave each of the children a hug. "I don't know what I would have done without you this week. You really saved the day."

"We like to help," Violet said.

Carmen gestured toward a table that had a wide, pink box on it. "I have a special treat to celebrate Pierce's release. I think Benny will really like it. Go ahead and open the box."

Benny ran ahead. He lifted the top off the box. "Cake! And it's decorated with an eagle." He grinned. "Pierce is happy *and* we get cake. This is the best way to celebrate!"

Read on for a sneak preview of

The Big Spill Rescue

**the first book of
The Boxcar Children®
Endangered Animals,
an all-new series!**

"I want to touch a shark!" called six-year-old Benny Alden.

"Shh!" Benny's sister Jessie put a finger to her lips. "The sign says we should whisper."

Benny put his hand to his mouth. Then he whispered, "I want to touch a shark!" just as excitedly, but quieter.

The Aldens were at the Port Elizabeth Aquarium. In front of them, a shallow tank stretched across the room. Inside, small sharks and stingrays swam lazily among rocks and plants. A sign above read "Touch Tank." That meant visitors were welcome to reach into the tank through the open top.

Grandfather put his hand on Benny's shoulder. "You'll get a chance, but first we have to learn the rules."

"That's right," said Isaiah Young. "Listen to Kayla, she'll explain."

Mr. Young was an old friend of Grandfather's. The Aldens were staying with him while they visited Port Elizabeth. Kayla, his daughter, was their unofficial guide to the aquarium.

"Thanks, Dad." Kayla spoke softly. "We whisper so we won't frighten the animals. You should also move slowly. Put your hand right under the surface of the water. Hold it there with your palm down."

The four children followed Kayla's lead. A stingray swam toward them. As it rose in the water, Violet's hand stroked across its back. She tried to keep quiet but let out a tiny squeal of joy and excitement. "It's smooth and slippery," she said.

"It didn't touch me," Benny said sadly.

"Be patient," Grandfather said.

"Are there other rules?" Jessie asked. She was twelve and liked to make notes about everything she learned. She couldn't write in her notebook with her hand in the water, but she'd try to remember what she learned for later.

"Don't try to grab the animals," Kayla said. "And don't try to touch their bellies or tails. Instead, touch their backs."

"What happens if you touch a shark's tail?" Benny asked. "Will it bite?"

Kayla smiled. "These sharks won't bite. There are about four hundred species of sharks in the world, and most are small and gentle, like these. You can handle them easily."

"We still need to treat them with respect," Henry said. At fourteen, he was the oldest of the Alden children.

"That's right," Kayla said. "We should treat all animals with respect. Here at the touch tank, the sharks and rays will hide if you scare them. But if you are calm and gentle, they'll get curious and come out."

"I don't want to scare them," Benny said. "I want to make friends."

Benny held his hand under the water. His body wanted to squirm, but he tried to stay very still. A speckled shark as long as his arm swam toward him. Benny held his breath. The shark nosed at his hand, and Benny got nervous. Then it slid past, letting Benny pet down its back.

"I touched one!" Benny grinned and clapped his hands together. Water from his wet hand sprayed into his face. He wiped himself off with his shirt sleeve as the other children laughed quietly.

After a few more minutes at the touch tank, Kayla asked, "Shall we move on?"

Everyone agreed. They were excited to see the other animals at the aquarium. After the children had washed and dried their hands, Kayla led the way to the next room.

Violet walked beside her. "We don't get to touch wild animals very often," she said. "I've been to a petting barn at the zoo, but those animals aren't wild." Ten-year-old Violet loved animals. She hoped she'd get a chance to draw some during their visit to Port Elizabeth.

"You shouldn't touch animals in the wild," Kayla said. "It can be dangerous. They could hurt you, or you could hurt them. The aquarium chooses animals that are safe for the touch tank, and the tank gives them places to hide if they feel shy. The workers also keep the tank clean and watch for any sign of disease."

They made their way into a glass tunnel. On the other side of the glass, water filled a huge tank. It felt like they were underwater with the fish! This tank held larger animals. Some of the fish were as long as a person was tall. At the bottom, crabs scuttled between sea urchins and coral.

Violet pointed through the glass. "Oh, that one is pretty. It looks like an orca, but it's too small. Is it a baby?"

"Hector's dolphins are the smallest marine dolphins in the world," Kayla said. "They are very rare and very endangered."

Benny frowned. "Are they in-dangered from people?"

"The word is *endangered*," Jessie said.

"Endangered means a species is at very great risk," Kayla said. "Only about seven thousand Hector's dolphins still live in the wild. If we don't help them, they might all die out. Then they would be all gone—extinct."

"That's awful," Benny said.

"Don't worry, Benny," said Henry. "Lots of people help protect animals like this. Right, Kayla?"

"That's right!" Kayla said. "There are many conservation groups that help. I work with one called Protectors of Animals Worldwide, or PAW."

Violet watched the dolphin as it swooped through the water. It swam close to the glass. Then it turned on its side, flicked its tail, and zipped away. It circled back around and wiggled as it passed by once more.

"It's dancing!" Benny said. He went up to the glass and started wiggling, trying to copy the dolphin's moves.

"You called this a marine dolphin," Violet said. "Marine means it lives in the ocean, right?"

"That's right," Kayla said. "Most dolphins live in the ocean, but a few live in rivers."

Benny spun around. "Will we see one of these dolphins in the ocean?"

"I don't think so." Kayla smiled. "Hector's dolphins live near New Zealand."

"That's on the other side of the world," Henry explained.

Benny sighed. "That's a long way. Maybe someday we can go."

"That would be quite an adventure," Grandfather said.

"I like adventures!" Benny raised his arms over his head as a sea turtle swam up to the glass. It looked like it wondered what Benny was doing. "We've had a lot of adventures," Benny told Kayla.

"Oh really?" she asked.

"It's true," Henry said. "We like to help people and solve mysteries."

"We like to help animals too," Violet added.

"I try to help animals," Kayla said. "I don't think I've ever solved a mystery though."

Benny smiled up at her. "That's okay. Maybe we'll find one for you while we're here."

Kayla laughed.

Grandfather said, "Don't be surprised if it happens. My grandkids always find something to get into."

Jessie pulled out her notebook. "Can you tell me more about conservation? It means trying to protect nature, right?"

Kayla nodded. "PAW has programs around the world. We try to save animal species, and that means we have to protect the land. After all, you can't protect animals if they don't have a safe and healthy place to live. Everything in nature is connected."

"What do you mean?" Benny asked.

"Say a factory dumps chemicals onto the ground," Kayla said. "The chemicals can wash into a river. They can flow into lakes or all the way to the ocean. What happens if you drop a plastic bag outside? It might blow miles and miles to the coast. It could get into the water and choke a sea turtle or seal."

"That's terrible," Violet said.

"We're always careful to throw away our garbage," Henry said.

"That's important," Kayla said. "Environmental groups like mine try to educate people on things like that. We work with local communities. We work with governments. Like I said, everything is connected. People are part of that web."

In the next room, penguins played in a large

area behind glass. They waddled across rocks and dove into a pool of water. Through the glass, visitors could see them swimming underwater. Violet plopped down cross-legged. She held her sketchbook in her lap and drew.

"We have African penguins and rockhoppers," Kayla said. "These are the African penguins. Rockhoppers have funny yellow feathers on their heads."

"They're adorable," Jessie said. "Are they endangered?"

"Sadly, yes," Kayla said. "Of the eighteen species of penguin, ten are endangered. Others are vulnerable. That means they aren't endangered yet, but there aren't as many as we'd like. Rockhopper penguins are vulnerable. African penguins are endangered."

The group spent some time watching the penguins, then Kayla led them outside, where a railing surrounded a huge pool. Inside were the biggest animals yet. "These are beluga whales," Kayla said. "They are found around Alaska and other northern areas."

The Aldens watched the three pale gray whales swim. One came close to peer at them. It had a bulging, rounded forehead. Its mouth seemed to be smiling.

"I thought whales were really, really big," Benny said.

"These are one of the smaller whale species," Kayla said.

Jessie read the sign. "They're still eleven to fifteen feet long. That's twice as long as Grandfather is tall, and the adults weigh more than one thousand pounds!" She made notes.

"I bet they have to eat a lot." Benny rubbed his stomach. "Like me."

"They are so cute!" said Violet.

Kayla leaned her elbows on the railing. "They sure are," she said. "I love coming to the aquarium to see the whales. But we can't forget about the animals that aren't as popular or as cute. All species are important."

"Right." Jessie looked up from her notebook. She thought she understood what Kayla was saying now. "Like you said, we are all connected. Bees pollinate many foods we eat. Snakes eat mice that would eat farmers' grain. Some people don't like bees or snakes, but we need those animals too."

"Every animal should be protected." Henry agreed. "Not only the biggest or cutest ones. I'd like to know how to help those other animals too."

The other children nodded.

Kayla smiled. "I have just the idea. But we'll have to leave the aquarium. Are you ready for a new adventure?"

"Always!" Benny said. "But maybe lunch and then an adventure, okay?" He rubbed his stomach again. "I'm hungry!"

GERTRUDE CHANDLER WARNER discovered when she was teaching that many readers who like an exciting story could find no books that were both easy and fun to read. She decided to try to meet this need, and her first book, *The Boxcar Children*, quickly proved she had succeeded.

Miss Warner drew on her own experiences to write the mystery. As a child she spent hours watching trains go by on the tracks opposite her family home. She often dreamed about what it would be like to set up housekeeping in a caboose or freight car—the situation the Alden children find themselves in.

While the mystery element is central to each of Miss Warner's books, she never thought of them as strictly juvenile mysteries. She liked to stress the Aldens' independence and resourcefulness and their solid New England devotion to using up and making do. The Aldens go about most of their adventures with as little adult supervision as possible—something else that delights young readers.

Miss Warner lived in Putnam, Connecticut, until her death in 1979. During her lifetime, she received hundreds of letters from girls and boys telling her how much they liked her books.